Ellie and the Secret Potion

Other titles in this series

Ellie and the Secret Potion

gillian shields

illustrated by helen Turner

BLOOMSBURY
CHILDREN'S
BOOKS

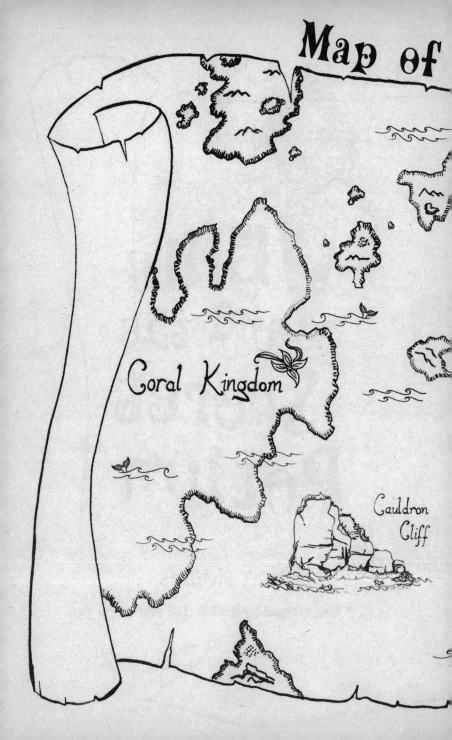

Map of

Coral Kingdom

Cauldron
Cliff

First published in Great Britain in 2006 by Bloomsbury Publishing Plc,
36 Soho Square, London, W1D 3QY

A CIP catalogue record of this book is available from the British
Library

ISBN 978 0 7475 8766 8

Printed and bound in Great Britain by Clays Ltd, St Ives Plc

3 5 7 9 10 8 6 4 2

All papers used by Bloomsbury Publishing are natural, recyclable
products made from wood grown in well-managed forests. The manufacturing
processes conform to the environmental regulations of the country of origin.

For Ophelia-Fleur

— *G.S.*

For my parents, David and Eileen —
thank you for all your support and
eternal optimism! All my love,

— *H.T.*

Prologue

Meet Misty, Ellie, Sophie, Holly, Lucy and Scarlett. They are mermaid Sisters of the Sea, who live in the magical underwater world of Coral Kingdom. The Merfolk and their wise ruler, Queen Neptuna, look after the sea and all its creatures.

Coral Kingdom is protected by six powerful magic Crystals, which give life and strength to the Merfolk.

Without the Crystals, Coral Kingdom would not survive.

Every year, the old Crystals fade and have to be replaced. Queen Neptuna sends Misty and her friends – six special mermaids who are pure of heart - to fetch the new ones from the secret Crystal Cave. But as they are bringing the Crystals home, a storm blows the mermaids completely off course.

This is no ordinary storm! It is created by Mantora, Queen

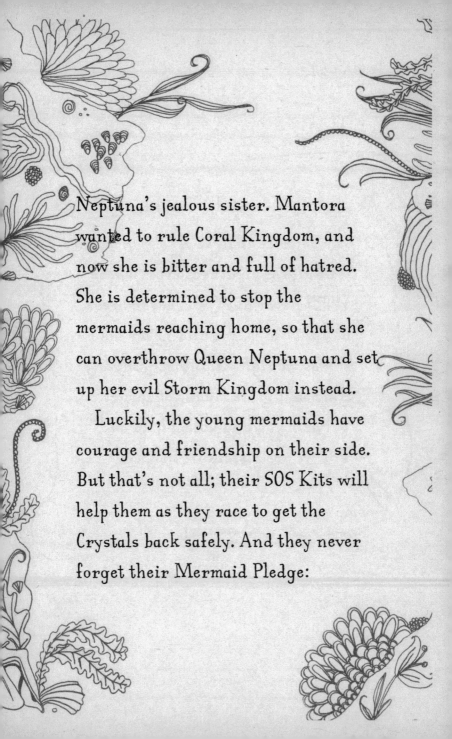

Neptuna's jealous sister. Mantora
wanted to rule Coral Kingdom, and
now she is bitter and full of hatred.
She is determined to stop the
mermaids reaching home, so that she
can overthrow Queen Neptuna and set
up her evil Storm Kingdom instead.

Luckily, the young mermaids have
courage and friendship on their side.
But that's not all; their SOS Kits will
help them as they race to get the
Crystals back safely. And they never
forget their Mermaid Pledge:

We promise that we'll take good care
Of all sea creatures everywhere.
We'll never hurt and never break,
We'll always give and never take.
And as we fight Mantora's threat,
This saying we must not forget:
'I'll help you and you'll help me,
For we are Sisters Of the Sea!'

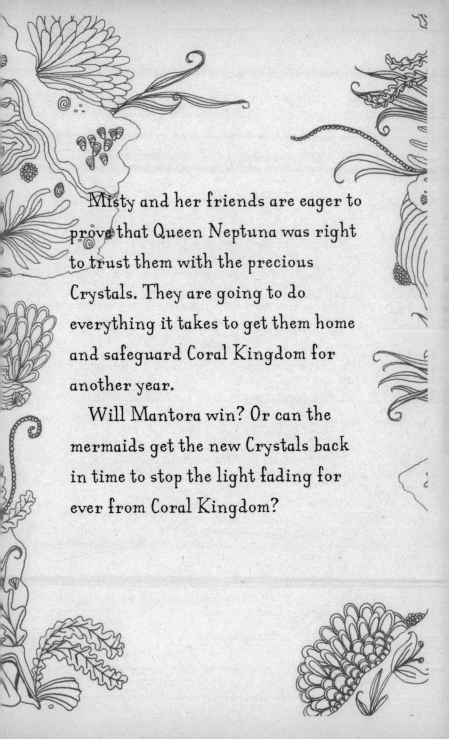

Misty and her friends are eager to prove that Queen Neptuna was right to trust them with the precious Crystals. They are going to do everything it takes to get them home and safeguard Coral Kingdom for another year.

Will Mantora win? Or can the mermaids get the new Crystals back in time to stop the light fading for ever from Coral Kingdom?

Ellie

Chapter One

'Wake up, everyone!' said Ellie, as she slowly yawned and stretched.

She had been asleep on a sandy island, but now the sun was coming up and making the sparkling waves dazzle her eyes. Ellie gracefully uncurled her glistening purple tail, then gently woke her mermaid friends – Misty, Sophie, Holly, Lucy and Scarlett.

'Ooh, I slept so well,' sighed Misty, blinking in the morning light. 'I was tired after our adventures yesterday.'

'I know, but we can't sleep all day, Misty,' smiled Ellie. 'Wake up, Sisters of the Sea. We've a long way to swim!' The sleepy mermaids rubbed their eyes and shook the sand from their shining hair.

Ellie and her friends weren't just going swimming for fun. They were Crystal Keepers, on a very important mission for Queen Neptuna. But two days ago, Mantora's terrible storm had blown the brave young mermaids miles off course to a deep Kelp Forest. And now they had to reach Coral Kingdom by the end of the

week, before it was too late.

'We must head West,' said Ellie, looking out over the dancing waves. 'That's where Coral Kingdom lies. But we just don't know how long it will take us to get there.'

Scarlett couldn't wait to dive into the cool water and set off.

'Is everyone ready?' she said impatiently. 'Then let's go!'

The mermaids slipped into the clear sea. Their tails glinted rainbow colours – red, pink, yellow, green, purple and orange, as they set off.

For a while they swam in silence under the cloudless sky, keen to get nearer to Coral Kingdom. Ellie glided through the water next to Sophie and Holly, their tails swaying up and down in perfect time with each other. Scarlett flicked her crimson tail eagerly and tried to edge ahead. Misty was behind the others, encouraging Lucy, who wasn't such a strong swimmer.

The sun was glittering on the waves and

a fresh breeze ruffled the mermaids' glossy hair. Then three snowy-feathered sea birds swooped above them.

'Look at those white terns!' Ellie said. She swirled her tail expertly and floated on her back. 'My mum says they are sometimes called fairy terns, because they look as light as gossamer. Oh, I wish I knew what it feels like to fly!'

'But we do, in a way,' Holly replied, as she glanced up at the elegant birds. 'Don't forget that Mantora's whirling storm blew us all the way to the Kelp Forest.'

'But that was rough and scary,' said Ellie, tumbling over to swim on her front again. 'I'd like to fly peacefully, like a white tern.'

'And I'd like to be a dolphin, riding the Wild Waves,' Sophie declared, as she arched her tail in a high, leaping dive.

Ellie smiled. Just for a moment she

forgot about racing home with the Crystals. She loved to see Sophie twist and turn cleverly in the water. Scarlett was a daring, graceful swimmer too.

'What about you, Scarlett?' she called out. 'Would you like to be a dolphin?'

But Scarlett wasn't listening. Her crimson tail whooshed through the waves, making a trail of golden bubbles. She wanted to prove that she could swim faster than Sophie, so she was racing ahead of her friends towards a tall rock. It stood up from the sea like a broken tower.

'Hey, Scarlett, wait for us!' shouted Misty.

As the mermaids tried to catch up with Scarlett, Ellie saw something strange. A magnificent Albatross, the king of the sea

birds, was flying overhead. But instead of gliding serenely, he was zigzagging around the column of rock and peering intently down at the sea. Ellie recognised instantly that something was wrong.

'Look,' she said to the others, pointing up. 'What do you think is the matter?'

Now the Albatross was crying out in a

harsh, deep voice. All the mermaids stopped in alarm, except Scarlett, who kept racing on.

'I'm swimming faster than any of you!' she called gleefully over her shoulder. 'I'm even faster than Sophie!'

As the stubborn young mermaid merrily sped away, Ellie noticed a dark patch gleaming on the surface of the water. It lay ahead of Scarlett like a menacing shadow.

'Stop!' Ellie cried out. 'There's something in front of you, Scarlett.'

'It's only seaweed,' laughed Scarlett, plunging through the waves faster than ever. 'You're such a fusspot, Ellie.'

Scarlett's vivid red tail flashed in the sunshine as she charged towards the shadowy water. But at that moment, the Albatross swooped down urgently.

'Danger! Danger!' he cried in his deep voice. 'Oil has been spilled in the sea ahead!'

Ellie instantly shivered at his words. Oil was very dangerous for all sea creatures – including mermaids.

'Be careful, everyone,' she shouted. 'We mustn't get a single drop of oil on our tails, or we'll be in real trouble.'

But it was too late. Scarlett had already swum into the dark, sticky mess…

Chapter Two

'Help!' Scarlett spluttered, as she struggled to swim back to her friends. What a shock the mermaids had when they saw her! Scarlett's delicate face was dirty and her hair hung in lank clumps.

'Ugh! I'm covered in oil,' she wailed. 'What shall I do?'

'You must clean it off straight away,' called the Albatross, as he circled

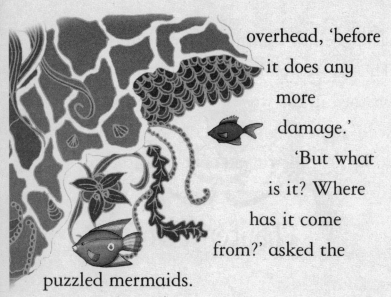

overhead, 'before it does any more damage.'

'But what is it? Where has it come from?' asked the puzzled mermaids.

'We bird folk have heard rumours that Mantora was here last night, with her snaky sea serpents,' replied the Albatross gravely. 'She is behind this trouble.'

'Mantora!' the friends cried. 'What happened?'

'A cormorant said that he saw a Human boat near that tall rock,' said the stately bird. 'A sudden storm blew up, as

sickly yellow lightning flashed in the sky.
The sea was boiling and dark shapes
writhed in the waves. Then Mantora's
scaly serpents pushed the boat against the
rock. The side ripped open, and the oil
tank flooded into the water.'

'So Mantora was using Humans again
to spoil the sea for everyone else,'
exclaimed Misty.

'When the sun came up there was no
sign of her,' the Albatross continued. 'The
Humans managed to get their boat to the
distant harbour, but look what they have
left behind!'

The mermaids stared in dismay at the
murky oil floating on top of the sea.
Scarlett was splashing and spluttering,
trying helplessly to shake the greasy mess

from her tail. But when she swam she felt
sick and giddy. She clutched on to Ellie
and started to cry.

'Can we do anything for Scarlett, Sir?'
asked Ellie bravely.

The wise bird looked down kindly and
said, 'Take her to those low green rocks in
the distance. You can tend to her there.
But now I need to fly and warn the other

sea creatures. Farewell!' He swiftly
wheeled away.

'We must get you cleaned up somehow,
Scarlett,' Ellie said.

'How?' Scarlett sobbed, her hair stuck in
tangles over her smudged face. 'Oil doesn't
wash off like ordinary dirt. I can't swim
properly any more and I feel so…so ugly.'

'Let's go to those rocky islands the
Albatross showed us,' suggested Ellie. 'It's
not too far.'

Ellie took Scarlett by the hand and
gently helped her to swim over to the rocks
and away from the oil. The others followed
them slowly. Then all the mermaids
pulled themselves out of the water, and at
last they were sitting together in the
sunshine.

The rocks were covered with fresh green seaweed and purple anemones. Gentle blue waves lapped against their sides. It would have been the perfect place for a Mermaid Party, if they hadn't all been so worried. Ellie was anxiously wondering how they would make it to Coral Kingdom in time if Scarlett's tail was damaged.

'I've got some Pearly Potion in my SOS Kit,' she said urgently. 'Has anyone else?'

The mermaids reached into their sparkly pouches and quickly found some soft sponges and dainty shell pots in their Kits. The pots were full of Pearly Potion, a magical cleansing ointment which glistened like fresh sea foam. The recipe was a secret guarded by the Merfolk.

Ellie and her friends dipped the sponges

into the sweet-smelling Potion. Then they carefully wiped them over the sticky smears and smudges. Soon, the Potion started to heal the blisters on Scarlett's tail. It really was Mermaid Magic! But Scarlett didn't enjoy being rubbed clean.

'Ow! Misty, you're so rough,' she complained.

'I'm trying not to be,' Misty replied, as she polished a rosy-red scale on Scarlett's tail.

'I'd love to give Mantora's nasty old tail a good scrub,' said Sophie grimly. 'Then she'd know what it's like to be smothered in slime like this.'

'Wasn't it a bit strange that Mantora was hanging around here last night?' said Holly thoughtfully. 'It feels as if she's

plotting against us everywhere we go.'

'I think Mantora did this on purpose,' exclaimed Ellie, 'so that she could ruin our chances of getting home in time.'

The others looked at each other in horror.

'Don't worry about being gentle any more,' Scarlett urged. 'Just hurry up so that we can set off again. We mustn't let Mantora stop us!'

Ellie and the others worked as quickly as they could. At last, Scarlett's tail shimmered like rubies, her skin gleamed and her hair shone like polished jet.

'You've all done a good job, but I'm glad it's over,' Scarlett sighed thankfully.

'Is your Crystal all right?' asked Lucy. Luckily, Scarlett's accident hadn't spoiled her twinkling Crystal, which had been hidden in her red pouch. The others quickly checked

their own Crystals, too. Then Scarlett slid
from the rocks into the cool waves. 'I can
swim again,' she cried happily. 'Now let's
go home!'

The mermaids got ready to follow her,
but Ellie hesitated.

'I hope nobody else makes the same
mistake as Scarlett,' she said, in a worried
voice. 'The Albatross won't be able to
warn every single creature.'

'We'll have to trust him to do his best,'
said Misty. 'Come on, Ellie, it's time for us
to be on our way.'

One by one the mermaids dived from the
green rocks into the shimmering sea. But
just as Ellie was about to follow them, she
noticed three bedraggled creatures
floundering on the waves. She gasped in

disbelief. They were the fairy terns she had seen earlier – but now their snowy feathers were drenched in black and sticky oil.

'Oh no,' cried Ellie. 'We've got to help!'

Chapter Three

Ellie dived into the sea like a speeding
arrow and raced towards the struggling
birds. Then she called, 'Misty! Sophie!
Please come over here!'

Soon all the mermaids were gathered
round the flapping, fluttering terns, taking
care not to go near the oil patch. The great
Albatross flew overhead again.

'Alas!' he cried. 'I was too late to stop

them landing here. But perhaps, Sisters of the Sea, you might be able to help?'

'We'll do anything we can,' Ellie said solemnly. This was her chance to do something for the bird folk that she loved. She quickly asked her friends to form a Mermaid Chain, strung out across the water all the way back to the sunny green rocks.

The mermaids carefully lifted and passed each fairy tern over their heads, one to the other. Soon the exhausted birds lay safely on the rocks, but they looked shocked and ill. The mermaids bobbed gently up and down in the waves that lapped softly against the little island.

'Now we must start cleaning their feathers, so that they can fly and look for

food again,' said Ellie.

'But we can't!' Holly replied.

'Why not?' asked Ellie, with a puzzled look on her face.

'You know I feel sorry for the terns,' Holly hesitated, 'and I'm angry that Mantora makes these things happen. But we've got to get back to Coral Kingdom.'

'She has a point, Ellie,' said Misty

slowly. 'Queen Neptuna is waiting for us.'

'And for the Crystals,' added Sophie.

'But we can't leave them like this!' Ellie
cried.

The Albatross had been listening very
carefully to the mermaids as he glided
above them.

'Mantora has caught you in a clever
trap,' he said. 'If you stay to help, you will
be slowed down in your task for the Queen.
Think how that would please Mantora's
black heart! Yet can you really leave these
helpless birds, brave Sisters of the Sea?'

'Oh, what shall we do?' groaned Ellie.

She felt torn in two by the difficult
choice. All the mermaids fell silent. The
delicate terns lay awkwardly on the rocks,
trying hard to stretch their wings. If they

weren't cleaned soon, they would not be able to survive. Someone suddenly broke the silence.

'We should try to save them,' said Scarlett firmly, pulling herself on to the rocks with a clever twist of her crimson tail. 'I know how horrible it is to be smothered in oil. These terns were flying as free as air, and now they can hardly move. Poor things!'

The others looked up, astonished. They had never heard Scarlett speak like that before. Perhaps Mantora wasn't the only one who would surprise them on this journey!

'But what about getting back to Coral Kingdom?' said Ellie in amazement.

'If we swim extra fast afterwards we can try to make up the time,' Scarlett replied stubbornly. 'We can even swim all night long if we have to. Anyway, aren't you forgetting our Mermaid Pledge?'

'We promise that we'll take good care…' Lucy began.

'… of all sea creatures everywhere,' finished Holly.

'That's what being a Sister of the Sea is all about,' Sophie said cheerfully. 'Scarlett's right, we must stay and help.'

The mermaids quickly joined Scarlett on the rocks and hugged her tight. She looked a bit awkward, but very pleased.

'Your Queen would be proud of you,' said the Albatross graciously. 'I will guard the sea to make sure this does not happen to any more of my folk.' He soared across the waves, calling, 'And perhaps we birds will find a way to repay you for your kindness and courage.'

Ellie squeezed Scarlett's hand to say 'thank you'. 'I'll never forget that you wanted to help,' she said.

'Well, don't get too excited,' Scarlett sniffed in reply. She had gone back to being her bossy old self again. 'There's still one tiny problem.'

'What's that?' asked Ellie.

'You used up every last scrap of Pearly
Potion on me!'

It was true. There was not a single
drop of the magic ointment left. How
could the mermaids possibly save the birds
now?

'I've got an idea,' said Ellie quickly.
'The ingredients for the Potion all come
from the sea. So perhaps we can make
some more ourselves.' She looked around
hopefully. 'Is it worth a try?'

'But what would we need?' wondered
Misty.

'Holly, your mum is a Healer,' said
Ellie. 'I know you help her to make
remedies at home. Do you remember what
goes into the Pearly Potion?'

'I'm not sure,' said Holly uncertainly.
'I've never made it on my own. I know you
need different kinds of seaweed…'

As Holly was frowning with
concentration, the biggest tern struggled
bravely to his feet. He bowed shakily to
the mermaids. His feathers were streaked
with sludgy oil.

'My name is Kai,' he said faintly, as the
mermaids listened eagerly. 'These are my

sisters, Ava and Skyla. Will you really help us with this mermaid Potion?'

Ellie looked at Holly with pleading eyes. Holly flashed back a sympathetic smile. 'We're going to do our best, Kai,' she said. 'But how did this happen to you?'

'We had been flying a long way,' he replied, 'riding the paths of the wind back to our island home, near these rocks. My sisters became tired, so they landed on the sea. I tried to pull them back from the danger, but we were all caught in the trap!'

'Try not to worry,' said Ellie, in a soothing voice. 'We'll make the potion somehow.'

'Thank you,' said Kai gratefully. 'But we are cold, so cold, even in this sun. My sisters were harmed more than I was. They are getting weak. You must make them warm – before it is too late. Please save them if you can!'

Chapter Four

'The Crystals!' said Ellie, with a snap
of her fingers. 'They are full of life and
light and power. Maybe they will comfort
Skyla and Ava until we can clean their
feathers?'

'Oh, Ellie, you are clever,' beamed Lucy.
'Let's hope it works.'

The mermaids quickly set their Crystals
in a circle around Kai and his sisters.

Glittering light shot out from the magical Crystals, like a ring of dazzling fire. It filled everyone with warmth and hope.

'Thank you, mermaids,' sighed Kai. 'That's better.'

Then Ellie and her friends looked expectantly at Holly, who had a faraway look on her face.

'Wait a minute, I'm thinking…' Holly screwed up her eyes as she thought hard. 'Hang on, I've nearly got it….Yes! I'm sure I know what to do.'

The friends listened carefully to Holly's hurried explanations.

'We'll have to search fast for the things we need. The most difficult one to collect will be the special, secret ingredient that has to go into the Potion. My mum told me about it once.'

'Ooh – what's the secret ingredient?' asked the mermaids. This sounded like a touch of Mermaid Magic!

'We need a pearl, given by the oyster who has grown it inside his shell,' Holly replied. 'But it will be hard to persuade an oyster to give his pearl away. Pearls take a long time to grow, so they are very precious.'

'That won't be hard for me,' said Scarlett bossily. 'I'll tell the oysters it's an emergency. They'll have to give me a pearl. I'll go and get one for you.' She started to uncurl her shimmering tail.

'Wait, Scarlett,' said Holly quickly. 'Perhaps it would be better if Ellie or one of the others went with you?'

Scarlett looked annoyed.

'Do you think I can't manage to get a pearl on my own?' she said angrily. 'I'll show you!'

'Oh, Scarlett, please be polite and friendly to the oysters…' Ellie started to say. But Scarlett dived deep into the waves and sped away without waiting to listen.

The mermaids looked at each other helplessly.

'Let's hope she really can find one,' said Holly. 'We'll have to collect all the other ingredients without Scarlett. But shouldn't someone stay with Kai and his sisters, and guard the Crystals?'

'I'll do that,' said Lucy unselfishly. 'I don't mind staying behind.'

Ellie thanked Lucy, then stroked Kai tenderly.

'We'll be back soon,' she whispered.

Ellie, Holly, Sophie and Misty dived like an arching rainbow into the sea, calling their thrilling rescue cry, *Mermaid SOS!* The race to make the Potion had begun.

'Do you see those sandy islets over there?' said Holly, swiftly leading the way. 'That's where we're heading.'

'What will we find there?' asked the others.

'Shells!' she grinned. 'They'll make the mixture strong to scrub off the dirt.'

The mermaids soon found themselves in the shallow waves near a sandy shore. Sparkling over the sand like a sprinkling

of pink diamonds were hundreds and
hundreds of tiny shells. A large yellow
starfish was basking in the warm water
which lapped gently against the beach.

'Greetings, Madame Starfish,' said
Ellie.

The starfish beckoned the mermaids over
with her waving arms.

'How can I help you, my dears?' she
said, in a friendly voice.

'We'd like some of
these shells,'
explained
Holly, 'but
we don't
know if that's
allowed.'
'Do they

belong to anyone?' asked Misty.

'No, my dear,' replied the starfish, settling comfortably on the sand like a plump cushion. 'These shells were left behind long ago by the creatures that lived in them. Some of them have even been crushed by the waves. You can help yourselves.'

Ellie and her friends thankfully filled their pouches with fragments of shells that glinted like slivers of glass.

'Are you making Mermaid Necklaces?' asked the starfish.

'Not today,' smiled Ellie. 'We're doing something much more important.'

'Oh, and what would that be…?' the starfish began to ask, but the mermaids had already dived back into the blue

waves, calling out gratefully, 'Thank you! Goodbye!'

'Well!' bubbled the funny five-armed creature. 'They were in a hurry and no mistake! It's made me feel quite tired. I think I'll just snuggle under this sand for a little nap...'

The mermaids were already racing along to find the next ingredient. It was like a Treasure Hunt, only it wasn't a game. The friends were determined to find everything they needed as quickly as possible. They dived to the sea bed like bright shooting stars.

'We should be able to find the seaweeds

that we need,' said Holly. 'Look! Those green and yellow ones right down there are just right for the secret recipe.'

Ellie sped downwards and stretched out her hand to pick a yellow frond from a bushy mound. But the next moment she let out a scream. The seaweed had spoken!

'What's all this, what's all this?' said a shrill little voice. 'Who do you think you're grabbing a-hold of?'

'I'm…er…sorry,' stammered Ellie, hurriedly letting go of the frond she had been clutching. 'Am I going mad, Holly? That piece of seaweed just talked to me!'

Holly laughed kindly. 'That's because it's a sea dragon!'

'Oh, of course,' said Ellie. 'I do beg your pardon, Mr Dragon.'

Ellie and the others stared hard at the swaying mass of green and yellow, until they could make out the shape of a slim pipe fish. He had wavy flaps branching out from his body, exactly the same colour as the plant where he lived. He looked just like a tiny dragon. Holly quickly told him what they were looking for.

'We need to take some of these fronds, if you don't mind,' she said, 'but I promise we won't try to take you again.'

'That's all right then,' the sea dragon squeaked. 'Gather as much as you need, just make sure you leave me behind!'

The mermaids thanked him politely. Then they shot away with a ripple of their glistening tails, clutching thick juicy bunches of seaweed. It was just right to make the Pearly Potion.

'I wonder how Scarlett is getting on,' said Ellie, as the mermaids surged up to the sunny surface.

'So do I,' replied Holly. 'If she doesn't get the pearl, all our efforts will be wasted.'

'Let's not worry about that yet,' said Sophie cheerfully. 'What are we looking for now?'

'It's right here in front of us,' said Holly. 'Fresh sea foam from the rolling waves!'

The others looked in surprise at the frothy bubbles that were churned up by the wind and tides.

'But how are we going to carry it?' puzzled Misty. 'It will just slip through our hands.'

It was a real problem. Ellie shut her eyes

and tried to think of what to do. But then she heard something overhead. She opened her eyes hastily and glanced up at the bright blue sky.

'Look!' she exclaimed 'I think help is near, after all. Can you see what I see?'

Chapter Five

Ellie pointed to where a family of pelicans was flying above them, chattering and calling to each other.

'Hi there,' she waved frantically. 'It's an emergency! Please stop!'

The kind pelicans glided down to the mermaids, who explained what had happened.

'Fairy terns, you say?' clucked the

mother pelican. 'Of course we'll help them.
It won't take us a minute to carry this
foam for you.'

The pelicans scooped beakfuls of the
creamy foam into their large pinky-yellow
bills. Then they flew to where Lucy and the
birds were waiting, followed by the plucky
mermaids darting through the waves. Ellie

noticed that the sun had begun to fade. In the distance, the magical circle of light from the Crystals glowed against the darkening sky. At last, the mermaids reached the seaweed-covered rocks.

'We're back, Kai,' called Ellie. 'We've got everything we were looking for.'

'Thank you,' whispered Kai, as he lay with his damaged wings protecting his shivering sisters.

'But we still haven't got the pearl,' muttered Holly. 'Where can Scarlett have got to?'

'Let's do what we can whilst we're waiting for her,' said Ellie.

So Holly showed her friends how to shred

the seaweed into pieces. The pelicans emptied their cargo of foam on to the fresh green mound, then flew away with the mermaids' grateful thanks. Last of all, the crushed shells were added to the mixture.

'But it doesn't look anything like the Pearly Potion,' said Ellie, as she stirred it doubtfully.

'Don't worry, it isn't finished yet,' said Holly. 'We still need Scarlett to bring the secret ingredient.'

Just then Scarlett's angry red face bobbed up from under the waves.

'Those horrid little oysters!' she said. 'They wouldn't give me one measly pearl. I told them that they had to, but they refused!'

'...er, Scarlett,' said Ellie, 'did you ask them nicely?'

'I didn't have time,' she snapped. 'I told them I was on a very important mission. That should have made them hand one over straight away. But they wouldn't!'

'It might have been better if you'd said "please",' said Lucy quietly.

Everyone looked at her in surprise. It wasn't like Lucy to speak up. Scarlett was just about to say something cross to Lucy, when she noticed all the mermaids looking at her with disappointed faces.

'So we won't be able to make the Potion after all,' Ellie murmured. She stroked the terns sadly. Scarlett began to feel rather

ashamed of herself. She looked away and
hung her head.

'I'm sorry,' she said in a small voice. 'I
see now that I said all the wrong things.
Oh, Lucy, would you go and ask the
oysters to give us the pearl? And you too,
Ellie? I'm sorry that I spoiled our chance of
getting one for the Potion.'

The mermaids had never heard Scarlett say 'sorry' to anyone before!

'Of course we will, Scarlett,' said Ellie, squeezing her hand. 'I know you tried your best. It's easy to make mistakes. But it's much harder to say sorry, like you've just done. Thank you.'

Scarlett looked a little bit happier.

'Tell the oysters that I said sorry,' she said. 'I mean, *please* tell them.'

'We will,' said Ellie and Lucy. 'Wish us luck! We'll come back as quickly as we can, Kai.'

They dived together through the clear blue water. The rocks that they had been sitting on were really the tips of some underwater hills. All sorts of colourful sponges and bright seaweeds grew on their sides. Tiny bright fish darted about. Ellie and Lucy swirled their sparkling tails and dived down further to the oyster beds. They wanted to find the pearl as quickly as possible.

The mermaids soon saw lots of little oysters nestled on the sandy sea bed. Their curved shells gleamed a lovely silvery colour. Ellie and Lucy hovered next to them.

'Excuse me…er…dear Oysters,' Ellie said nervously. 'If you don't mind, we came to ask you about your pearls.' A hundred oyster shells opened and a hundred angry little oysters glared at the mermaids.

'HANDS OFF OUR PEARLS!' they shouted. The oyster shells snapped shut. Ellie tried again.

'But we only need one, to help our friends Kai and Skyla and Ava,' she said.

The oyster shells opened a tiny crack.

'That bossy mermaid with the shiny red tail said we had to give her all our pearls.' Then they suddenly closed tight!

'She didn't really mean that,' said Lucy quickly. 'Don't think badly of her. She wants us to tell you that she's sorry for being bossy.'

One by one, the little oysters opened their shells and peeped out.

'Apology accepted,' they said. 'But we still won't give our pearls away. They take a very long time to grow.'

'We know your pearls are very precious,' said Ellie patiently. 'We wouldn't ask you to give us one just for ourselves.'

'What's it for then?' asked the biggest oyster suspiciously.

'It's to make Pearly Potion for some fairy terns who are covered in oil,' Ellie replied. 'Mantora tricked the Humans into spilling oil into the sea, by getting her sea serpents to smash their boat against the tall rock.'

'Humph!' said the oysters. 'We don't trust that greedy old Mantora, or her ugly sea serpents. She'd love to steal all our pearls if she could.'

'We're doing our best to fight Mantora and her selfish grabbing and greediness,' said Ellie. 'Could you bear to part with a single pearl to help us? Then the birds will be able to fly in the sky again.'

The oysters seemed to huddle together, whispering to each other. After a few moments, a little oyster at the front opened his shell wide and spoke up.

'Do you mean there really is a SKY?' said the little oyster. 'Is it all big and blue and high up? We've heard about it, but we've never seen it. We always live down here, you know. If you take me to see the sky, I'll give you a pearl.'

'Of course we will,' smiled Ellie. 'We'll gladly give you a ride to see the sky.'

All the oysters cheered as Ellie lifted up the little one and sat him on her shoulder.

'HOORAY FOR OLLIE!' they shouted. 'He's going to see the SKY!'

Then Ellie and Lucy flicked their shining

tails and headed for the surface. The
sunlight from the Overwater world made
the water glow as the mermaids raced to
join their friends. They had succeeded in
finding a pearl after all. Now Ellie would
soon find out if the secret ingredient really
would work.

Chapter Six

The mermaids all fussed over the little oyster, as Ellie and Lucy gently placed him on the rocks.

'Thank you for coming,' said Scarlett shyly.

Ollie gazed up at the sky. It was a beautiful greeny-blue, streaked with a red sunset.

'Ooooh!' he said. 'There really is a sky

after all. It's so big and high. And so
many colours! It's the most...
splendiferous ... thing I've ever seen. Of
course you can have a pearl. I'd have given
TEN pearls to see this!'

He seemed to huff and puff for a few
seconds. Then a perfect pearl popped out of
his shell on to the rock. It was exactly
what the mermaids needed.

'Now if you'd kindly take me home,'
said Ollie, 'I want to tell
the other oysters all
about the big sky.
And I need to
start growing
another pearl
straight away.
That's what we oysters

love doing best. Goodbye! I hope the terns get better!'

Lucy smiled and picked him up carefully. Then she dived into the water to take the little oyster home.

Ellie dropped the pearl into the mixture as Holly stirred it. Then something amazing happened. A shimmering haze rose up, like a soft white cloud. When the pearly cloud disappeared, the mixture had changed. Instead of being a green sticky mess, it was a rich Pearly Potion. The secret magic of the pearl had transformed it.

'Holly, you're a star!' cried Ellie. She gently rubbed the pearly cream all over Kai, whilst the others looked after his sisters. The dirty oil soon melted away like

a bad dream. By the time Lucy came back from the oyster bed, Kai's beautiful white feathers gleamed brightly. He wasn't a bedraggled creature any more, but a dazzling fairy tern. Ava and Skyla stood next to him, shining and graceful.

Kai nuzzled his beak against Ellie's hand in thanks. The air was full of the birds' happy cries. The magic circle of light from the Crystals leapt high like a ring of fireworks, as the white terns flew joyfully into the evening sky.

'Hurray!' the mermaids laughed.

'How can we thank you, Ellie?' said Kai, as he swooped round her. 'You have saved our lives.'

'Really?' said Ellie, with starry eyes.

'Really and truly,' replied Ava and Skyla. 'If you or your friends ever need the

bird folk, just call and help will come. We know you delayed your journey to Coral Kingdom, so that you could save us.'

Coral Kingdom! Everyone at home would be waiting for them. The mermaids quickly packed the bright Crystals away and started to think about the journey ahead. But as Ellie hid her Crystal carefully, she was still worried about the oil patch. What if other birds landed on it? As she was closing her pouch, the Albatross flew overhead.

'Thank you for all your help, mermaids,' he cried. 'And I bring good news. The Humans who spilled the oil from their boat are sending a rescue team to clean it up.'

'I never knew Humans did anything

like that,' said Ellie. 'I'm so glad.'

'So am I,' said Lucy quietly. 'I think that some of the Humans love the sea as much as we do.'

'But we don't want any Humans to find us here, even if they do care for the sea. It's time to go,' said Misty.

'We really will have to swim all night to make up for lost time,' added Sophie. 'We've spent a whole day here!'

'I'm pleased we stayed to help,' said Scarlett firmly, 'even if it does mean a tiring journey for us now.'

But at that moment a wonderful sight filled the evening sky.

Great sea birds flew over the rocks in teams of four, all holding strong ropes of seaweed in their beaks. Each set of four ropes was attached to a giant clam shell, lined with mother-of-pearl.

'You may ride in these shell carriages tonight, brave Sisters of the Sea,' called the Albatross. 'It is our way of saying thank you. We will carry you until dawn, so that you can sleep. Then we must return to these rocky islands of ours, to make sure that Mantora does not come here again. By then you will be rested and further on your way.'

The mermaids thanked him over and over again. They each climbed gratefully into a smooth shell, which made a perfect mermaid bed. Then the Albatross teams slowly flapped their strong wings. The seaweed ropes which they held in their beaks lifted the shells into the air. The mermaids skimmed quickly over the waves, as the moon rose high in the sky.

Ellie's wish had come true. Now she really knew what it was like to fly!

Kai and his sisters flew next to the mermaids, calling out in their silvery voices;

> *Now you'll fly free,*
> *Under the stars with me,*
> *Yes, you'll fly free,*
> *Over the land and sea.*

Ellie, Misty, Holly, Lucy, Sophie and Scarlett softly joined in the song.

We are sisters of the sea,
Flying like birds so free ...

The mermaids would never forget helping the terns, though they were relieved to be on their way again. They were more determined than ever to get the Crystals home safely to Coral Kingdom.

But as the brave young mermaids were lulled to sleep by the sea birds' song, they didn't know that Mantora was lurking below the waves, plotting against them once more. They couldn't guess what adventures the new day would bring to the Sisters of the Sea...

Mermaid Sisters of the Sea

Misty has flowing blonde hair and a shimmering pink tail. Misty is a really determined and brave mermaid.

Ellie is very caring and loves sea birds. She has long, wavy dark hair and a glittering purple tail.

Sophie has funky fair hair and a blazing, bright orange tail, which helps her to swim super fast.

Holly has sweet, short black hair and a dazzling yellow tail. Holly is very thoughtful and clever.

Scarlett has fabulous, thick dark hair and a gleaming red tail. She can be a little bit bossy and headstrong sometimes.

Lucy has fiery red hair and an emerald green tail, but don't let that fool you – she is really quite shy.

By the same author

Misty to the Rescue

gillian shields

Ellie and the Secret Potion

gillian shields

Sophie Makes a Splash

gillian shields

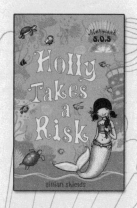

Holly Takes a Risk

gillian shields

Scarlett's New Friend

gillian shields

Lucy and the Magic Crystal

gillian shields

**To order direct from Bloomsbury Publishing visit www.bloomsbury.com/gillianshields
or call 020 7440 2475**

www.bloomsbury.com